Vivid Entries:
"Where Words Come to Life"

Robert Issac Polk

Poetic City Presents

Robert Issac Polk often performed poetry at Ice Event Center.

-Is it Love?-

Maybe if I hold my breath
Maybe if I held love over sex
Maybe if I ever gave my respect
Maybe you and I wouldn't second guess
Is it love?
Is it us?
All these arguments kill my buzz
When we're too proud to give a fuck
When it's too clouded to even trust
When the world is louder than both of us
Is it love?
Is it us?
Maybe if I hold my breath
Maybe if I held love over sex
Maybe if I ever gave my respect
Maybe you and I wouldn't second guess
That this is love.

-5 Steps in-

I know that it's times when I can make you sad
I know that sometimes I can fuck up
and that's my bad
But through it all I love you
and you love me
We were never meant to be perfect
only take steps to being worthy for us to be
We we're 5 steps in
5 steps into love, trust, communication
respect, and being friends
I'm not trying to move backward
Only shed light on what matters
Step into a future of you and me
Prevent the past
make the present anew
Make a future where just love will do
Step by step
I'm not trying to rush it
but if we fall
Just know I will pick us up every time
No discussion
5 steps in
Devoted
Ready for marriage
You as my focus
Ready to carry you as my token
Ready to defy every odd
no matter how hopeless

5

My path has been chosen
On me, you can depend
Because I'm already 5 steps in

-Sapiosexual-

I gave her a piece of me that she desired
She wanted my brain
My words she admired
Working my tongue as she envisioned
All of my words with definition
I performed
with each moment
she was more and more involved
I was eating away at her walls
That she opened up to me
She said I touched her deeper than deep
I pierced her soul and it was poetry
Please don't stop
Right now, I'm her rock
She hasn't felt like this for months
So I went harder
I performed
Hell! I put on a show
Just so she would know
my words were more than just a post

-Black is Beautiful-

All the colors of the rainbow can't define you
You're more beautiful than they are
must I remind you
While your personality
hits every color in the spectrum
It was the color of your skin
that put you closer to perfection
Black is beautiful and beautiful is black
I'm not hating on the rainbow
but that's where it seems to lack
it's just the facts
So while they're chasing rainbows
looking for gold
I made a fortune off of oil and coal

-The Craft-

It's a craft in the action
Love your work
Make it yours
That's a passion
Relationships are art never mask it
It's always a lesson to the past shit
We explore, we critique, we get better
I guess the common goal is forever
Just looking for a soul to make me better
To put me on a whole 'nother level
I stay hoping that I'm good enough
I stroke you
Praying that you love my touch
A blank canvas
I'm hoping I can fill you up
Just like magic turn us both into something
There's no perfect road that we can explore
So we can just get lost wanting more
I have never been so sure
Name on my chest yeah that's yours
My name on your breath wanting more
The love I confess that it soars
I'm looking in your eyes seeing stars
Doing everything I can to take us far

It's a craft in the action
Love your work, make it yours
that's a passion

Relationships are art never mask it
It's always a lesson to the past shit
We explore, we critique, we get better
I guess the common goal is forever
Just looking for a soul to make me better
To put me on a whole 'nother level
We kiss
We kiss to get it perfect
Loving what we do, so we're working
Nothing more to prove
Who we hurting
If I'm in love with you
Why they worried?
Is it the way I stroke you with intentions?
Write out our adventures
Poke you to submission?
Because I swear it's out of love
As long as you know the truth
Why should I even give a fuck?

-None of it Feels Real-

The emptiness won't hold me
Vacant is my arms
Trying to imagine who I'm holding
None of it feels real
I just want the feel of one-touch
Thinking to myself like
Who could I love?
Who could I trust?
I wish I could rush and decipher feelings
However temporary doesn't heal me
Eager souls don't feel me
I just want you to hear me
Who stops to listen?
My visions are sad and lonely
They want me but they don't want me
They don't try to get it
Because who pays attention?
No vision of the future, past or present
Like we didn't learn our lessons in love
Yet, they still eager to fuck with no emotion
Try to hold me with no devotion
When I already fucking told them
The emptiness won't hold me
Vacant is my arms
Trying to imagine who I'm holding
None of it feels real
I just want the feel of one-touch
Thinking to myself like
Who could I love?

Who could I trust?
When none of it's real
I guess I'm just waiting
on that day to be fulfilled

-Remedy to my Love-

I wish you would come
and give me head for no reason,
Just because you feel like it
not because I'm needy
Come, climb all up in my center
That's baby
Act as a woman should
so when they ask, *is that yo girl?*
I'd say naw that's my lady
I want to argue with you
have you drive me crazy
Know that it's all out of love
because we laugh about it daily
I want to take a picture of you
Carry it around in my wallet
Just for the hell of it
Just to say I got it
Trust me
I'm not trying to be a problem
I just want a love I can fall in
Start it up, no stalling
Answers when I'm calling
Gives the best sex that I ever had
Catches me when I'm falling
Appreciates talking
The silence
Someone who is trying to go the distance
without being concerned with the mileage

Because it's all about the memories
That love type love
That's the remedy

-Love-

Faith in love
Thinking will I be her one
So crafty with her tongue
That I sacrificed my sons
I took her blessings
So many sessions
Just gave my heart more questions
I marveled in her presence
Took her mind and stripped it naked
Made love to her essence
I was her possession
She claimed all of me
All of my affections
All of my imperfections
Gave my mind direction and made it heaven
I swear head is a blessing
But it doesn't hold a candle to being accepted
Not by who you love
Sex is just sex
But kindred souls soar when they fuck
Allowing each other to go deeper
She is my teacher and so I preach to her
She moves as I move beneath her
To love and not deceive her
We are one
And to me that is love

-The Difference-

I can't say that I never had a good woman
We just had too many problems
and I wasn't ready to be the difference
We absolutely could have made it
I just didn't give it the attention
I was worn and not ready for the war
I was stupid enough to believe
That we had nothing to fight for
in fact I was sure
But I admit that I wasn't right
If I could go back now I would fight
Maybe change our lives
Make better decisions
No matter the outcome
I'd be sure to be the difference

-My Queen-

From beyond this bed of mine, I see
You on top, melanin tone, white tee
Hair so thick it won't ever fall down
Above your brows the essence of a crown
In your walls, I bury my life seed
Deepened moans your nails inside of me
Grinding slow your body so profound
On this dick, I vow that heaven will come down

Close your eyes my energy you'll see
Feel my touch yet visualize my being
With this sweat, I work to make you proud
Overtime if you keep it good and loud
I slap that ass I swear it sway in circles
Say my name let's strive to keep it verbal
With that headboard, I stay on beat
Nice and deep applying pressure to your clit

Say my name like you never been so sure
Claim this dick and make it truly yours
Marks on my body for everyone to see
That last night I was deep inside my queen

-I Wonder-

I wonder if I killed you
because I never had forgiveness
Sometimes I want to die
I can't handle the stress of all my feelings
I know I made you cry
I reflected all my pain
Never did I try to make you feel bad or the same
I just wanted you to understand
Even when you tried to make it up and love me
I could never comprehend
I just kept you at a distance
That hurt even more
Every time I saw you I'd be sore
Only fighting with myself
I was too proud to admit I needed help
Steady killing myself by stressing over fails
That I was no longer right
in mind and body I was ailed
sickened by my limits
praying that they see my intentions
seeking out forgiveness
I can't say that I even deserve
because all the times I could have forgiven
I left you hurt

I wonder if I killed you
because I never had forgiveness
sometimes I want to die
I can't handle the stress of all my feelings
I know I made you cry
I reflected all that pain
so maybe it's only right that I feel the same

-Exhausted-

I wake up exhausted
tired of all the bullshit
still taking losses
How can I fucking trust
When my hearts screaming caution?
When you're inconsistent as fuck?
Steady taking pauses
You're not here
I don't think what you want is all that sincere
Because I don't feel the dedication
I want you to take me seriously
Like your college midterm
Study and fucking ace me
I can't seem to keep your attention
You treat my very mention of time like a lynching
What's the point of feeling lonely?
When you're here
You don't even hold me when you're near
I'm asking for consoling but do you hear?
We will never persevere
You wonder why the fuck I stay clear

-Living in the Moment-

Civil twilight in the morn'
Wrapped up in your arms
For your love
I will reform
You're the best
Steady sleeping on the rest
Heart pounding out my chest
For your love, I am so blessed

Just kiss me
Say you love me, baby
I have been waiting for the moment
to drive you crazy

Just kiss me
Say you love me baby
I'm just living in the moment
We don't have to fall, just rise
I've been shopping for a ring
that's about your size
All I need is a queen that's mine all mine
Who can dream with a king and waste no time
On one knee with pride

Just kiss me
say you love me baby
I've been waiting for the moment
that I drive you crazy

21

Just kiss me
Say you love me baby
I'm just living in the moment

Civil twilight in the morn'
Wrapped up in your arms
Spreading love and giving warmth
Flesh to flesh
Heart banging through your breast
Hands upon your hips
pressing firm against your lips

Just kiss me
Say you love me baby
I've been waiting for the moment
that I drive you crazy

Just kiss me
Say you love me baby
I'm just living in the moment

-The Real Me-

We don't always get it right
I majority get it wrong
But I never lose the insight
So many things we take for granted
Only when we lose it
We find understanding
This world is so demanding
I lose self
Have to be selfish enough to keep me
So I lose help
It's all a fucking trade
Even in my worth, I get played
They don't see my fucking value
I get overlooked for the best parts of me
Like we're not all fucking fallible
Like my feelings can't be actual
Because you don't understand
Or like when you categorize me
for being a man and not who I am
I just want you to see me
Not the world that has hurt you
Not my past that I try leaving
The real me behind the fucking picture
If you have ever known me
Then you would know
It's not all about the visual

-We Are The Monsters-

We are the monsters
Awful still no better than our fathers
We treat women like
we have no respect for our daughters
Lambs to the slaughter
We steal and we barter
We praise God's work
Yet have no respect for the artist
A woman's worth in any description is modest
Yet somehow we took something so flawless
We made it human downplaying the goddess
Now all we're stuck with is fake
Disloyal, and dishonest
We just relate better to carnage
We find more comfort in the imperfections of others
If I'm being honest
As man, we destroyed our women
By making them lose faith in all of us
We are the monsters

-All of Because-

I used the love to hold her back
Told her lies, gave her dick
When I owed her stacks
Kept her lost
Couldn't find the truth with an almanac
She had the proof
Just loved me too much to see exact
I see my fucked up ways
Yeah, I'm the one to blame
I see your heart has changed
I can't even say a thing
In your absence, I live madness, life's dramatic
I'm no savage
I'm just asking for love
I know past actions make it harder to judge
You're not falling for trust
You're not falling for us
And it's all of because
I used the love to hold her back
Told her lies, gave her dick
When I owed her stacks
Kept her lost
couldn't find the truth with an almanac
She had the proof
Just loved me too much to see exact
I see my fucked up ways
We haven't talked for days
If we did, I'd say

I know I made some big mistakes
Though my heart may break
I know I got some shit to face
It's harder when I'm starving just to see your face
When love can't be exchanged
You're not falling for trust
You're not falling for us
And it's all of because
I used the love to hold her back
Told her lies, gave her dick
When I owed her stacks
Kept her lost
couldn't find the truth with an almanac
She had the proof
Just loved me too much to see exact

-Can I Judge her?-

How the fuck do I walk away?
Every time I try
it's a memory, not in one, am I a saint
So can I judge her?
Every time I try
I find out just how much I love her
I can't leave
Hell, I got to fight for something
I'm just tired of my friends
calling me a stupid motherfucker
All these interventions
People on the outside looking in
Trying to take my relationship and lynch it
Like, what the fuck?
I guess I'm the only one who ever been in love
Contradicting bitches
If you can't respect that I'm fighting for my family
then just mind your fucking business
Or tell me
How the fuck do I walk away?
Every time I try it's a memory
Not one time, am I a saint,
So can I judge her?
Anyone who says I can
is a stupid motherfucker
Because every time I fuck up
I see just how much she love me
She ain't never walked away

So I'm going to be just as dedicated
I'm going to choose to stay

-One Touch and You're Lost-

What is love?
But a purpose
When it seems so worth it
When it seems so certain
You don't need any words
You just feel it all
Deep breath and a pause
One touch and you're lost
Moist you lose poise
a little inner voice got you throbbing at the source
So you take my hand
Put it down your pants
Apply so much pressure
I kiss your lips
Bite your neck
You get so much wetter
Playing with your clit 'til you cream my hand
Brush it on your tits suck it off again
Strip you out your clothes loving all that skin
Up and down I kiss
I lick
I get high off love like this
One hit
One motion
One sound
We moaning
Got damn
I own it

29

I pound
I pound
I pound

What is love?
But a purpose
When it seems so worth it
When it seems so certain
You don't need any words
You just feel it all
Deep breath and a pause
One touch and you're lost
I got lost in your inner you
Touching your outter
Your heart be the pinnacle
Every time that you splatter
Can I go deeper?
So deep, that I'm deep in you
Tell me how do you feel
when I'm all that's eating you
My hand at the center of your back
Deep breath and a pause
One touch and you're lost

-Perception of a Side Chick-

She said I can love you better
And she may be right, now
but I know she's not forever
She doesn't have my dedication
I strip you down to your soul
to pull out your admiration
Just to watch you stick it in
And as deep as you shove it
I never break, run, or bend
I take it
The pain and the pleasure
I stand here naked
every second of this love for you
to know that I'm forever
Wondering if you see me
Whisking away your problems
like your own personal genie
Trying to make that bitch go poof
And if you think I'm lying for a second
You being here is the proof
Using my touches to soothe
What's left of the heartbroken
Until I'm who you choose
I'll just play the role of the unspoken

-Killer Mindset-

So stuck in that killer mindset
We dead
I tried to give her the world
All she wanted was head
Thinking the whole world was out to get her
I tried to step out with her
She says you ain't my nigga
I consider you a friend
But later can you hold me
We can cuddle, and stay in
Fuck me like you own it
Damn I know you want it
Trust me I'm not the girl you belong with
Killer
So stuck in that killer mindset
We dead
I tried to give her the world
All she saw was red
Too worried about these other bitches
She called fake but made real
After all, I wasn't her man
but she be damned if she lost me to them
So she figured
She would make me her nigga
Just to control the things around me
Before they got any bigger
When she didn't even really want me
She would rather settle with a lie

than to ever be lonely
Killer
So stuck in that killer mindset
We dead
I tried to give her the world
All she knew was bad
She pushed me away so many times
I fled
She had no one to run to
She burned her bridges with everything she said
With all the lies that she told
After while she didn't even have me to hold
I had to let her go
we were too gone, we were dead
And she owes it all to that killer mindset

-A King-

I hold you tight
With a smile that burns bright
And in my mind
I think your still the greatest being
My life could ever bring
A king to my soul as the world will soon know
That you're my child
I'm proud to help you unfold
To a life full of things
A world full of dreams
That in time will help you to see
What life means to be free
Free to love
Obtain the knowledge of a lifetime
So through your mind
You will never find the weakness to be blind
Only speak your mind
Let your character define
The power and will
For the greatness you hold inside
Never let anyone take what lies
Deep beneath a heart that tries
Pride is glory and you hold glory inside
To elevate your mind
To find that family is always united
In some kind of form or fashion
It will always be delighted
To find that I can be there

somewhere in your greatness
Every moment I'm away
I find that moment to be wasted
So with much anticipation, I'm faced with
The greatest glory in life
I could ever be blessed with

-Pyromaniac-

I'm here because she burned me down to nothing
Left me with the suffering
All I did was love her, stoked her flame
so it wouldn't smother in her heart
For a while all I got was sparks
Until she burst and all I saw was dark
She spread across my plain
left it smoldered, hot to the touch
that never kept me from trying to hold her
I could take her sizzles
but never any of her burns
She took a toll on my family
when they realized my back would never turn
Over time they learned
Just to leave me in her ashes
They called me pyromaniac
Because my flame was my passion
Fire isn't that easy to contain
Yet I swear that she's my flame
I hold her and all I endure is pain
But before the blaze
There's this spark of glory
Then ashes to ashes on all I see before me
I'm a pyromaniac

-Brown Skin-

Brown skin is a beautiful complexion
A smile that drives me wild
Her mind, so intelligent
You see there's no need to ask
What brought you to my attention
Because through words
I could give you no response
Even in poetry
Passion couldn't be written
That describes my love for you
Just to know that love is destined to glisten
Brings me furthermore into the essence of you
Furthermore into the deep passion
Of making love to you
Through good or bad times love is soothing
When love holds the right mind to choose
Understand its use and values
Never wanting to hold another
Never losing your trust
Because of the words of others
There is no need to worry about lust
Love has well taken over
From the first moment I held you
And confessed that loving you is my closure
From the first to the last strand of your hair
To grow gray and get older
I would be there to hold you
Making sure you know that I love you

While I console you
I could never be worth anything
Without you knowing that one thing is true
Brown skin, I love you

-My Finish Line-

What kind of man doesn't see you as an angel?
I prayed for you, I told God thank you
How blessed could I truly be?
He sent you
You gave me seeds
Put a piece of me on this Earth
I can't help but know your worth
I'm unworthy
Making you a believer is the first thing
Taking you as my wife to make it life is for certain
It was God that made you earthly
Your mind that made you worthy
Beauty most certainly
With a desire to love instead of hurt me
That's why I love you
I know through your sacrifice we soar
It's your love that brings us joy
Makes my heart love more and more
Each and every day
You're the reason I know my God listens as I pray
The reason I fight for another day
The reason I find no reason
To ever look the other way
I'm only running to what's in front of me
You are the only prize behind my finish line

-Black and White-

I looked at you and saw black and white
The bigger picture
The in's and outs of my life
I know it's probably too much to ask of a friend
I could marry you before we even begin
Silhouette of what we were
Tell us dreams of what's to come
I think I fell in love
In the middle of that talk 'til the morning sun
Day by day I'm falling more
I ask my heart to just be sure
You know if I didn't know any better
I'd swear that you're the one for me
I'd hold you down forever
I heard that friends do it better
So let's take this thing we got
Amplify it 'til I can't measure
Love, you know I never judged
You were there for me
So I accepted who you was, that was us
Birds of a feather
You were five stars
So you know it was a pleasure
I promise, I never thought I'd see the day
Where I man up and said I loved you
Not in the friendly way
Hey, I'm thinking maybe you should stay
I'll be your friend tomorrow

Just not the one I am today
I looked at you and saw the black and white
The bigger picture
The ins and outs of my life
I know it's probably too much to ask of a friend
But I could marry you before we even began
A silhouette of what we were
Tell us dreams of what's to come
I think I fell in love
In the middle of that talk till the morning sun
Day by day I'm falling more
I ask my heart to just be sure
I hope you know that I would love you
In that moment
Truth be told before then
I'd practice all my vows
In case I cried I'd record it
No way they'd miss our story
We were best of friends before this
In my heart, I had a dream
It was destined to move forward
Bells, under the archway I stand still
Watch you walk on down that aisle
Vera gown, Weitzman heels
Damn sexy, look at you
I pinch myself just to see
But before I wake
I do

-Before I Cry Myself to Sleep-

She would cry herself to sleep
I was there
Listening about the man
That would cheat and have affairs
I would comfort her, tell her it would all be okay
Not knowing in the morning she would go back
She would stay
About a week later
I would finally get a call
I would say how you been
She would say not well at all
My heart has been broken and I was just hoping
I had a friend and that your door was open
She would come and cry herself to sleep
I was there
Listening about the man
That would cheat and have affairs
I would comfort her and tell her it would all be okay
Not knowing in the morning she would go back
She would stay
About a week later
I would finally get a call
I would say can I see you
She would say no not at all
I can no longer tell you how I've been
or how my hearts been broken
I can no longer call you friend
or even come at your door hoping

But only take this time
To tell you that it's over
Before I cry myself to sleep

-Kindred-

She bonded with my soul
we so kindred
That relationship kind of arose
before we befriended
Made promises to never let her go
my mother be my witness
As I took her hand from her father
after I asked his permission
Decisions, dates
conviction that it's the fate that brought us here
Practicing my vows with the man in the mirror
Daydreaming that I hear her say, "I do"
I break a smile
I didn't even know that she walked into the room
I'm astounded,
I return the gesture by telling her "I do"
to me, we were just married in that room

She bonded with my soul
We so kindred
That I never let her go
I made her misses

-I Want it All-

All of my wishes came
In the form of dreams that eluded me
Craving the sensation of a love
not tainted or diluted of its purity
I sought for something whole
I took in her breath with kisses
Only ever to complete a goal
I wanted life
But only found mere substitutions
We make love
The love we make creates tension
Never an opportunity
Am I selfish to want it all?
I climb and yet I fall
I master her inner walls
Yet get lost behind our flaws
Suddenly it's hard to see the light
It grows ever so dim
Until its completely out of sight
Despite my love
Though love doesn't seem to be enough
We try our best to hold on
In all honesty we just fuck
It doesn't fill the void
Even when I say I love you
No matter how true, it doesn't bring you joy
Yet you yearn to hear it
To be alone we fear it

The idea of love is the obsession
Even though our paths point
Two different directions
We stand stagnant
I just want to move forward
I honestly don't know
If it's you that I move toward,
Yet we lock lips in a manner
that makes your pussy lose poise
Moans and screams through the night
make you lose voice
So much passion that it pulls
and makes it feel like we lose choice
All of that love and aggression
Wrapped up in sheets that are too moist
It always ends in I love you
As we proceed to walk away,
Apparently, I'm too selfish to stay
I want it all

-Whenever You Come Walking My Way-

I still hear that melody play
Whenever you come walking my way
My heart starts booming
In sync with the way you be moving
I fell so in love with the music
I kiss you, I lose it
So perfectly tuned, it got to be
True artistry in motion
Or at least that's what I told me
It's symphonies when you hold me
The silence when I'm longing
Please don't be too long
It's been forever since we danced
I've been waiting to take your hand
Let's go, Let's kiss
Let's just hold hands, let's be like this
Just please don't stop the music
I don't think that I can lose it
So in love when we're moving
So in sync, it's fusion
I still hear that melody play
Whenever you come walking my way
My heart starts booming
In sync with the way you be moving
I fell so in love with the music

-What She Wrote-

Love is what she wrote
Fingers pressed upon my back
As she caressed me with every stroke
Kissing, writing notes like all mine
Fingering her pussy just to ink the dotted line
We official
Made the deal as I kissed you
For this love that feels so visceral
It goes deeper
I Sleep, fuck, and eat you
It's a need
Deep inhales when I breathe
I get lost in you and me
It's open seas
Fuck the way back
She cumming as I came back
It's a puddle where we lay at
But we cuddle after great sex
Open arms
So thankful that I'm yours I reform
Great you, great me
Great pussy, great D
I cater, I eat
On haters, we sleep

Love is what I wrote
Singing in the shower as I lathered her with soap
We so dope, that we fuck and people quote

Check the post
Full of passion
All the love that fills my actions
I don't substitute, nor mask it
If I'm in it then I'm smashing, full devotion
I sailed her waves, my ocean
On this dick, she is coasting
Full of focus, hocus pocus
Got no shame when she deep throat it
She wet it, keep it soaked
Even when they're quoting this
I doubt they hit my notes

-Up, Down-

We go up, down
Close your eyes for the visual
I'm Pushing in your mental
So deep that I can feel you
I've been pressing out your issues
No time, no we don't stress
Hands beneath your dress
A constant dream I must confess
Girl we go up, down
Licking on your clit
All of me inside your lips
Hand pressing on your hips
Girl don't you run, no don't resist
You never came, not quite like this
I got that brain, I'm on that shit
All you keep saying, you want that dick
Girl we go up, down
Ride it, damn
That pussy so profound
Every position, every sound
Pushing deep inside your mental
So deep that I can feel you
Steady pressing out your issues
No time, no we don't stress
Stripped you out that dress
Nothing on but your best
Kissing on your flesh
I swear I love that ass to death

I will be your hero, fuck your ex
I got that passion
Got that depth
No looking back
No retrospect
Just you and me
No need for a next
Girl we go up, down
I can love you like I love you
In the bed, I'm prone to fuck you
Nice and freaky is a must-do
If you bold, that's a plus too
I'm sold on just us boo
This dick will make you bust true
In your pussy, in its muscles
When you flex I swear I love you
All your stress is in your puddle
Keep it coming, got damn
We go up, down
Ride it, damn

-What It's Like-

What it's like to fall in love
A lonely you trying to call it us
Personal truth trying to call it just
No clue, so you call it trust
But is it real?
Can't speak for the other
So you go off of how you feel
Doing all you can, trying to make the shit appeal
Trying to sell them on a dream
But you're selling them surreal
Baby, love has never been ideal
But true will of steel and even then you deal
Trying to reach loves zeal
It's a bitch of a journey
Even true love leaves you sickened and hurting
Have days when it's fuck it
and you're closing the curtain
Have days when you love it
and the shit is all worth it
Love is only you and how you see it
It's never who you're with or how they're being
People love to talk
But what the fuck are they saying?
Love is your art
Don't let a motherfucker paint it
Know your worth and get acquainted
It will all work out
Trust in your experience

Fuck word of mouth

-Truth Hurts-

I don't see a way out
But you get in
I can't get you to stay out
Feeling more stupid
The love is all played out
Every time cupid wins
I can't even say get out
I'm stuck in this up and down
Back and forth bullshit
That keeps me spiraling out of control
Been trying to let go
Only God knows why I hold on
My free will feels so far gone
I'm walking on eggshells
For a motherfucker who doesn't respect me
My heart doesn't protect me
Thoughts of my kids won't let me
Feeling like my very soul is in jeopardy
No matter how much I try to do right
Smile as I kiss my kids good night
Then I cry myself to sleep each time we fight
My prayers don't set me free
Shackled by my inner voice
That still clings to maybe
While you survive on the mercy of one last time
While I kill myself over you on a daily
Always jeopardizing my peace of mind
Like I want to live this way

You can't even tell me why it is this way
I can't even understand why the fuck I stay
I try to talk about my feelings
You blow me off with a quick okay
You're not even listening
So finally I stepped out
I was tired of being the victim

-Heat Rated R-

In the moment of heat
You don't have to speak
I just want to hear you moan
Clinch my body when you peak
Deliverance by the grace of tongue
Come and take a seat
Sit you on your knees
Let you grind it 'til you're weak
At ease
Clit sensitive appeased
You don't have to run
You know I got my needs
Pussy lips I feed
Dive until she streams
Release your body of its load
Then we breathe
We turn seconds into hours
All your stress has been devoured
I beat the pussy until it trembles like a coward
She trickles and she showers
Yeah, that's multiple orgasms
Breathe
It's almost over
Now she's looking for closure
So I pull her closer
As I whisper sweet poetry in her ear
As I steady fuck her in her pussy
I nibble on her ear

She don't worry
She knows her nigga so sincere
The only thing I fear
Is my message being unclear to others
Because I fuck her like I love her
The evidence just squirted on the covers
Breathe

-To Silence The Thoughts-

I want to silence the thoughts
I'm so tired of being awake
I want to sleep when people sleep
Feel normal but I can't
Violated by my memories
Exhausted by the worries
Haunted by my loved ones
Praying to God for mercy
I can't see my purpose
Thinking about love
Maybe if I never hurt her
She would be the one
Thinking about my children
My daughters, my sons
Wondering if I can be a better father
Hate I wasn't when I was young
I don't like regret
But can't help but think about changes
I wish I had kissed my mother more
Been more thoughtful, less angry
More loving, less hateful
More confident in me
Strong enough to face my truths
At peace enough to sleep
But regrettably, I'm not
So until next time, it's back to my thoughts

-What I Believe-

I can only tell you what I believe
How God sent you from Heaven
Designing you for me
How stars turn to wishes
To get them you must believe
All these years a slave
It was love that set me free
God who devised the plan
Then me, steady wishing
for a single person to understand
I believe
That after being down for so long
he sent you to pick me up
Knowing that I would fall in love
Knowing that I would care for you
the way you care for me
Knowing the way I feel for you
is how it's meant to be
Knowing that we would strive
As long as I believe
Through trials and tribulations
I never gave up on love
I knew I needed patience
Failed attempts made me better
Having faith kept me centered
My God knew I needed preparation
Before you entered
Called me fickle

During a time where love spoke in riddles
I finally understand enough to get you
I perceived
Finally enough to love you
That's what I believe

-Born Again-

How can something meant to fulfill
Leave you hollow?
I tried a dose of love
Nearly overdosed on the bottle
Too good at times
I couldn't seem to get enough
When that shit brought me down
I knew I was truly fucked
Too addicted to leave
Too broken to stay
Too far from my God
So how can I pray
All I have is this love
So I begged for it
He tried to walk out
I grabbed his legs for it
I was sick
I lost my family when I named him it
How can he push me away?
Knowing that this is all I have
Knowing that I have no choice but to stay
I overdosed
I killed my life behind this addiction
When he couldn't give a shit that I was in love
We were indifferent
I was a victim
Love was my killer
Wielding a man I thought was my healer

I died
I left that life behind
I found god
I found a new me
Every day I pay my respect
To the woman
I will never again be

-The Moment-

Love is a defining moment
Especially when you want it
Might change your life's components
Take a nigga make him honest
Love is worthy
It's me and you emerging
As one
You're an extension of myself
When I breathe, you take a breath
When you hurt that shit is felt
Can you imagine
That I love you with a passion
Every action, satisfaction
When you're gone it's something lacking in my life
So I rather make you wife than miss a moment
I rather love you right
Then to live lonely
My only
Love is optimistic
I swear we're not statistics
I got in and made an entrance
Now I'm saying fuck the visits
Without you, I'm so livid
Picture perfect, we so vivid
Happily made a commitment
Now we shacking no resentment
The Moments

-Fuck me?-

She says fuck you because it hurts
Damn, I truly love you
Just been wondering what it's worth
I sacrificed, I put you first
You don't even notice
Yet you wonder
Why we're out here looking hopeless
I don't give a shit about your friends
If it ain't benefiting us that shit's pretend
I'm not about to run and hold your hand
If I can't trust you
It's fuck you
The end

Fuck me?
Hell, I sacrificed too
It's me that holds us down
It's me that gets us through
You always ready to quit
Over some insecure ass shit
If I didn't change myself
you would have been done and left
I walk on eggshells just to make you happy
I don't even recognize this man
It's all husband, all daddy, I love it
So why you over there on your fuck me
It's me who comes home
To make you love me

It's me who makes you smile
and changes the subject
So smell my dick and check my phone
Afterward, treat me like I'm the one that's wrong
But what you won't hear me say is fuck this
Because even with yo' bullshit I love this

-Fuck'em-

You know I burned so many bridges in my time
I could never get across to anyone without preparing
For some climb
No point of view of mine
Was ever wanted or needed
So I dwelled in the, *"told you so"*
Whenever I could speak it
Fuck'em
You know grass is always greener on the other side
But where I stand I'm at home
Yeah I'm in mine
I never dwell on the past
Unless I got the company to travel back in time
Because looking back from where I came
I would say I'm doing fine
Living free
I've purposely burned bridges to my history
By telling them to exit
Simply don't come visit me
Fuck'em
I'm so far from nothing
That I turned my life around
Just about reached something of my own
Call it what you want
But don't call me on the phone
Just so you know I'm disconnected
To be left the fuck alone

-Do You Love me?-

Why is love used as a dumb-ass question?
Am I not so invested that?
I have to waste my time securing your insecurities
Just to make you my own
And if my heart is so much of a place
That you require
Then why don't you know
That a house is not home
A relationship is not a throne
And that my feelings are not my own
Until they are freely expressed
Instead, you choose to live in a world
Where opened wounds were never dressed
Where your body steady protest to know
That us making love is more than sex
Me fucking you is just for show
Yet you still have the nerve to question
Was it the sex talking
Or was it your affections
Like we have no plans for the future
No directions
This only makes me question
How deep is your love
When it's vested to the point
Where you still have doubt
I'm just curious to see
Do you love me?

-Temporary-

All these temporary people
Temporary comforts
Temporary equals
Looking for the real thing
Is like that haystack with the needle
If you couldn't be the one
You will never be the sequel
Damn is anybody truly gleeful
While I was searching for potentials
Hell, I stumbled on deceitful
Now I'm searching for credentials
because I rebuke the evil
If your not the type that's needed
Then I will never need you
Who the hell am I suppose to plead to?
Far from perfect
But I am not beneath you
Bitch I'm peaceful
Fuck your evil

-Queen-

How stupid could he be?
To have you as a woman
and disrespect a queen
There is no honor in a commoner
You deserve the finest
That nigga not a man
Just ignorant and blinded
He knows he doesn't deserve you
That's why he cracks under pressure
He will never be your equal
Just continue to be your lesser
He is nothing but a lesson
So you can call it fate
A step in the right direction
A journey to something great

-The Most High-

I woke up with the most high
Went to bed with a dream
Didn't want to close my eyes
But the scratches let me know it's real
When you fucking with a star
That's how it's suppose to feel
Through her darkened tunnel
I could see her light
Sex be so good that she start to bite
I fell in love with her overnight
She kisses me like she misses me
and never said goodbye
She just came and she came
Puddles in the bed I just stood in the rain
Puddles on my head and my head remains
Head game, no game, coldest thing
Put her right to sleep
I just starred for a minute
Not a sound, not a peep
I woke up with the most high
Went to bed with a dream
Didn't want to close my eyes
But the scratches let me know it's real
When you wake up to no one
How you suppose to feel?

-Pieces of You-

With a shadow of a doubt
I think I broke you
Me and every other nigga
You gave all of your hope to
I use to think damn she so beautiful
Even within
Now the only thing beautiful about you
is the cover of your skin
It's like you lost a piece to your puzzle
All I want is it returned
I'm not trying to judge you
Only speaking on concern
Maybe give you closure
You were always right
I'm sorry I never told you
That as beautiful as you are
I never fell in love with the out
But the in
Just to make you whole again
I'd give you back every piece that I can

-Real Woman-

It goes like this
I don't give a fuck
I wish I never been in love
This is why it's hard for me to trust
You never were the one
I fucking hate you
I should of
But I never did because I ain't you
You're a fucking fool
I was good to you
You're going to shut the fuck up and listen
Fuck them bitches
You're not going anywhere
Stay away from my fucking children
You made your decision
You didn't want us
You not a fucking man you just a little boy
To think I trusted you with my heart and more
That's the last time you hurt me
You'll never see my tears
I'm deserving of a real man
Real woman here

-Not Right Now-

I haven't allowed myself
To truly want a person in forever
Too many complications
With trying to mix two life's together
Like what's your plans for the future?
How do I even fit?
Nine times out of ten I don't
I'm just what's right now
That's why I even exist
I'm just here because you stuck right now
You don't even want to make love
You just want to fuck right now
I'm steady asking you what's up right now
You always answer with not right now
Why not right now?

People tell lies
Just to get in a broken heart
Got no respect for others
Not even from the start
They say they been hurt before
So why share that pain?
But dish out that very emotion all the same
Selfish in all of their tendencies
I wonder if it's all on purpose, if it's meant to be
I once asked, *do you know stress be killing me?*
You replied, *if so then why don't you leave?*
I'm here because I'm stuck right now

You don't even want to make love
You just want to fuck right now
I'm steady asking you what's up right now
You always got to answer with not right now
Why not right now?

You make excuses
Like you sell bullshit for work
Lucky me I guess I get it first
Had to let it go, even tho it hurts
Hold out for something new
and pray for perks

Status single
So you mad as fuck right now
Tripping because I'm not stuck right now
You don't even want to fuck right now
You on that let's make love right now
You say can we talk right now
But I'm like no, not right now
No, not right now

-I Kiss it Make it Better-

Your pussy overzealous
I fuck it and I swell it
Grinding in my face
No need for umbrellas
I kiss it, lips get jealous
On your face nothing to tell them
Hell, I kiss it to make it better
I kiss it to make it better
Moans go acapella
Headboard beat they go together
Swear that beat it goes forever
That beat goes forever
On your tongue, I start to swell up
Girl you on a different level
I watch you and I revel
I watch you and I revel
In that pussy I go feral
In that pussy I'm the pharaoh
Pussy tight girl it's so narrow
Swear I'm trying to be your fellow
Yeah, I'm trying to be your fellow
Like Hello
Slap it watch it move like jello
Make me sell my soul, you devil
Pussy should warn to be careful
But I work back in like Mello
So deep you want to tell all
But hell naw

Your pussy overzealous
I fuck it and I swell it
Grinding in my face
No need for umbrellas
I kiss it, lips get jealous
On your face nothing to tell them
Hell, I kiss it to make it better
I kiss it to make it better

-All The Love You Ever Gave-

I was wrong about you it's that simple
All the love you ever gave, detrimental
Too many years a slave, too sentimental
I only viewed the love in my heart, no fundamentals
For you, I made myself a cripple
You were just so fickle
That I never knew
If the love in your heart was supplemental
Mentally uncivil, sinful
Judgemental
Killed me a little everyday
Shit I start to dwindle,
Pistol at my temple
Suicidal to my mental
Thinking dear Lord
What the hell did I get into?
BANG

-Poet of 3005-

It's funny how we're stuck in time
Words are immortal, try writing a line
I have been writing for the poets of 3005
Tell him to snap for me, keep me alive
Take a piece of my mind
I donate it
A bit of my pain might shape you
Love is a claim that people cling to
You got to be smart
To read the angles
It's an effort in love
Some think it's for sale but they never the one
If love is all hell then it's practically done
Let it die with the moon
Get back to life by the sun
A little wiser
Love denies us
To teach
About the real one's we meet
I hope you never lose one
They play hide and seek
Meaning very hard to find
I hope you got queens in your time
Approach with how you feel
Ain't no need to use a line
It's a 50/50
Play the odds in love
And never regret what the outcome was

It's funny how we stuck in time
Words are immortal, try writing a line
I have been writing for the poet of 3005
Tell him to snap for me, keep me alive

-All I Took for Granted-

I wish I would have told you
That I didn't need the bike
That I appreciated the candles and the books
Whenever we went without the lights
That cable was nice but honestly
I liked our walks so much better
That I much rather you be home
Than slaving to buy me unneeded pleasures
I miss our movie nights
Just chilling watching old flicks
I wish I would have taken up your offer more
Instead of hanging with temporary friends
I miss the birthday dinners
The never-ending calls, the hugs
I miss you being there
Through all of my problems, whatever they were
I miss our talks, our laughs, our love
I miss the idea of you walking through the door
Now I'm just expecting you to come
Sadly you never do
So I just wait thinking
Of all I took for granted with you

-The Moment-

Love is a defining moment
Especially when you want it
Might change your life's components
Take a nigga make him honest
Love is worthy
It's me and you emerging
As one
You're an extension of myself
When I breathe, you take a breath
When you hurt that shit is felt
Can you imagine
That I love you with a passion
Every action, satisfaction
When you're gone
it's something lacking in my life
So I rather make you wife than miss a moment
I rather love you right
Than living lonely
My only
Love is optimistic
I swear we're not statistics
I got in, made an entrance
Now I'm saying fuck the visits
Without you, I'm so livid
Picture perfect, we so vivid
Happily made a commitment
Now we shacking no resentment
The Moments

-Pique My Imagination-

Come pique my imagination
I just want a dream with a queen
for me to escape with
You can exaggerate a little
This is that go big or go home
Let's promise to never make it simple
Because I won't
Hell, I super duper love you
And when it's just us
Hell it's super duper us two
And Fuck them if they don't see it
They can all stay woke
While we're dreaming
Happy as ever
Still together
Fuck them and their relationship failures
I'm too involved
With making dreams that much better
Making smiles so bright
That they can soak up typhoons
So in love got me writing haikus
Love is blind
But I hear you
Never deaf to the visual
I see everything even when I'm asleep
I stay woke
Even in my dreams
I have hope

It's just you and me
Two souls
Beyond that is motherfuckers just trying to impose
Fuck'em
They never wanted us to make it
So Fuck'em
They never understood how far we would take it
So Fuck'em
I hope that our love makes them sick
The cure is on the tip of my dick
Pique my imagination

-The Thought-

The satisfaction of knowing
That I am what you're thinking about
Really turns me the fuck on
So much that I push aside this thong
I think about us too
All the things we do
Like the way that you touch me
Sensation still lingering
From the last time that you fucked me
Thoughts still tingling from
When you told me you love me
That I have to touch me just to feel your embrace
I want to know everything that you felt
So I even taste what you taste
I get lost in myself
So lost that I don't want any fucking help
Unless it's coming from you
The music in the background guides my moans
So elegant the tones
That I hope you hear me
But I'm so close to this nut
That I could give a fuck if you don't
Pussy so wet that I highly doubt if I don't
Just bust all over these fingertips
My only regret is that you didn't get a single drip
I'm not stingy
Just lost in the thought of you in me

-Purpose-

I could dream a dream though not as perfect
Laying up in your melanin awaiting to surface
The skin I'm in so delicate no way to word it
I could swear I touched your soul
And it gave me purpose
I think you're reflecting on me
Tonight I fell in love with your melody
I watched your body play
The distinct sounds it made
Like the moans that come and fade
That orgasmic pitch
That raised and slowed the tempo
Never grip me gentle
You don't hurt me
I won't hurt you it's that plain and simple
Let's get comfortable just chill
Pull me close, closer
Close enough to love you and get deep
Sex and conversation
No sleep
I think I loved you in a past life
This chemistry we're feeling is so pass life
Take a look, there are our bonded souls
In a sea of matrimony with that promise to hold on
Girl, you honor me,
In the bed, beyond the sheets
I don't give pillow talk my credit
because I'm deep

Feel beyond my being
And see my means
I'm not talking about what's in my pockets
In those polo jeans
My hearts affected
By the curve of you invested
That smile you do, majestic
It's so easy to obsess with, I know
I have never been in love like this before

I could dream a dream though not as perfect
Laying up in your melanin awaiting to surface
The skin I'm in so delicate
No way to word it
I could swear I touched your soul
And it gave me purpose

Listen
Twin flame we the same soul
I fell in love on the day
I couldn't let you go
You mirrored my very essence
In a sense that made me whole
Kissed my lips left me breathless
In that minute, I was froze
At that moment I was sold
Standing next to my blessing
In a tale yet untold

-So in Love-

Trying to talk is the battle
Shortly after feeling like do we really matter
Or should I just say fuck it
You know I think it's funny
How we can hate and can love them
How it's such a thin line
To be so in love
and still feel like you're wasting your time
The shit drives me crazy
Because when you're here I want you gone
But when you're gone
I'm saying, *babe, when you go be home*
Don't leave me alone
I need you next to me
Then they climb in bed
And you start questioning
You go to war with yourself
Like am I really this pathetic
That I can't do it by myself
Do I love you that much
That I will sacrifice my health
Where did I lose me?
Then you spend days on in lying to yourself
Looking in the mirror saying shit like
"I choose me"
But it just never happens
So in love
The funny thing is you've never been happy

-Silly Bitch-

Tell me where would we be
If I didn't give a fuck or no energy
Why do we fall in love with the enemy?
Fuck the chemistry if there's no synergy
This is my contemplation
You can shut the fuck up
Keep your conversation, fuck being stuck
Got no time for waiting
You pressed your luck
You tried my patience
Bitch how stupid you think I is?
I ain't your toy or your fucking kids
Ima handle my fucking biz
Depart from whatever the fuck this is

When you see me, don't know me
Or ask nothing on me
Not friends, not homies
Nor need your consoling
I'm pissed!
Tricks are for kids silly bitch!

Lie after lie you tell
You pussy rich,
But no longer can pussy sell
Pussy bitch, its a lack of interest
I fucked you at the top of business
Now you just slanging visions

Wishing somebody would claim yo' hoe ass
It's not my class to save you
I rather just hate you and leave you for sadist
Hope you ain't atheist
So the good lord can take you,
That's his biz
While I depart from whatever the fuck this is
and please

When you see me, don't know me
Or ask nothing, on me
Not friends, not homies
Nor need your consoling,
I'm pissed!
Tricks are for kids silly bitch!

This Life is Not The One That I Want

Why for real love
Do we have to work the hardest?
While the people we fuck with
Never are the smartest
Beautiful but her tongue slick
I swear that she's a goddess
I can't take her nowhere
Unless it breaks my pockets
This one that says she loves me
Why is she so crazy, another who just fucks me
I swear she wants my babies
but none that I can trust
I swear the shit is crazy
out of all of this, all of u,
You would think I have it made, but I don't
This life is not the one that I want

One that gave me all her tears
Gave me all my babies, all her kids
I replace it for all my sins
Time wasted that we can never get again
She was patient while I was out there getting it in
Truth be told she will never be the same
Truth be told I fucked up
I'm to blame
Now we can't even trust each other
Trapped and smothered
Still saying I love you,

But truthfully I don't…
This life is not the one that I want

I look at me, I look at you
Mirror, mirror I can't determine who is who
On some real shit
I would like to up and say I do
So why am I killing it
With every other bitch I screw
I'm a fuck up, absolutely no luck
I know I'm weak
I woke up hoping I wouldn't show up
But here you are, there I am
Again and again
So hey
I want to trust you
I know that I can't
hell, I won't
This life is not the one that I want

-All the Pieces of You-

Too many pieces to the puzzle
So he just gets frustrated and leaves
Not realizing that each time
He takes a piece from you
Not realizing that he's the disease
The very reason that you can't pull your shit together
All he does is take
You're so quick to give
Day after day you break
You cry
You look in the mirror-like who the hell am I?
The crazy thing is you'll never know
Because you let him walk out with your pride
Shit on your identity and fuck your mind
Putting your all into your children
Because you look for them to pick up the pieces
Believe me, they'll try
But they can never make you whole
Because they didn't break you down
To be honest, neither did he
You gave yourself so freely time and time again
When you should have said fuck you
And put it to an end
You should have saved yourself
Now it's my job to piece together all that's left
The fucked up thing is
I don't know where to start
because I've only known this broken image

And that bitch walked out with the box

-All The Things You do-

You make me feel like it's magic
All this nigga do is bring madness to you
But you never break or bruise
All you ever do is stay true
Your love, your strength, it's so apparent
If you ever got a real man I could imagine
All the things you could do, you would do
Thinking of all the things I could do with you
You're always working
always serving
He doesn't deserve it
When you're deserving
I swear that I could be so good to you
I swear that I could be so good for you

You make me feel like it's a habit
Beautiful, carrying the weight of the planet on you
courageous in all that you do
Thinking why the hell are men such fools
Your love, your strength, it's so apparent
If you ever got a real man I could imagine
All the things you could do, you would do
Thinking of all the things I could do with you
You're always working
always serving
He doesn't deserve it
When you're deserving
I swear that I could be so good to you

I swear that I could be so good for you

-Perspective-

Making love to your flesh
Is addictive in a sense I obsess
I mean you don't know what's real
Until you fucking with the best
If pussy could kill I would swallow you to death
Wrap up in your arms it would never be a next
Girl, I'd give you all of me if you'd accept
I'm asking solemnly and with respect
I'm done swiping to the left
Girl I'm trying to take your heart and your breath
Wake up every morning with perspective
If you ever wondered why
I sleep facing your direction

-I'm Mine-

I ain't for you
You ain't for me
Love for us was just a lesson learned waiting to be
A brief moment in time
That I was yours, you were mine
But I'm sure we'll turn out fine
Let's just praise another day without lies
Drinking to the why's
Excuse me if I cry
But I stand empty inside
What used to fulfill me
Tried to break my heart and kill me
But somehow I made it
Just to stand here and say this

I ain't for you
You ain't for me
Love for us was just a lesson learned waiting to be
A chance at a new life
I think I'll take it
But this time I won't let you break me
This hate in my heart it ain't me
So I'm going to take my time in saying
That I forgive you
I love you and I will miss you
That we will be just fine
Because today I'm no longer yours
I'm mine

"Rest in love, family."

- Bennie Gang
est. 2015

Robert was an amazing person.
He was passionate about family, friends, and
poetry.

He never met a stranger, and made everyone
feel safe and free to express themselves without
judgment.

From his battle with cancer as a child,
to his battle with medical issues as an adult,
Robert's focus always remained on everyone
else's well being.

Robert was a man of many talents,
but most importantly,
he was a son, father, brother, nephew,
cousin, lover and friend.

He will truly be missed by many.
His poetry was his story....and you will feel it.

I love you little bro. Always and forever,
no matter what...see you on the other side.

- Dana Ball, Sister

www.ingramcontent.com/pod-product-compliance
Lightning Source LLC
Chambersburg PA
CBHW050413030726
47503CB00006B/2168